Teacher's Read-Aloud Library

Why the Jackal Won't Speak to the Hedgehog

Naja the Snake and Mangus the Mongoose

Rumpelstiltskin

City in the Summer

Santiago

Perhaps

Naja the Snake and Mangus the Mongoose

Naja the Snake and Mangus the Mongoose

A JAMAICAN FOLKTALE Written by Oliver Kirkpatrick

Illustrated by Enid Richardson

Doubleday and Company, Inc., Garden City, New York

This special edition is printed and distributed by
Scott, Foresman and Company by special arrangement with
Doubleday & Company, Inc., 277 Park Avenue, New York, New York 10017.

"I am the last living snake in Jamaica," Naja the Snake hissed with pride.
"I know," Mangus the Mongoose snarled, showing his deadly sharp teeth. "We mongooses were brought here all the way from India to kill snakes. Now only you are left. When I kill you, our work will be finished."

Naja was calm and haughty. "Then you'll have no more snakes to fight. What will you do? Lie in the sun and get fat?"

"You'll never live to see that," said Mangus. He was purple with rage. But he was too tired to attack again. So he waited and watched.

The gentle motion of Naja's head floating from side to side began to hypnotize him.

Suddenly Naja hissed.

Mangus jumped. He had been dozing. How easy it would have been for Naja to bite him with her poison fangs.

"Fight," Mangus snarled, and launched himself with the speed of a bullet at the poised head of the snake. He came so close that his sharp teeth cut Naja's skin behind the neck, but she quickly darted out of his reach.

Mangus ran headlong into the tree behind Naja and fell to the ground. It was all he could do to roll out of the reach of her deadly fangs.

He turned quickly, his eyes on Naja. If she would only move away from the tree, Mangus would not have to worry about running into it again.
"Move away from the tree," Mangus snapped.

Naja only smiled and stayed in front of the tree. Mangus kept trying to attack. He ran this way and that, back and forth, but Naja moved so that the tree would always be behind her.

At the end of the day, Mangus was so tired he could hardly stand.

"Are you tired?" Naja asked with a smile.

"Of course not!" Mangus said.

He lay on his belly for a long time, resting. He had been doing all the running, and his legs hurt. Even his tail hurt. And he was hungry.

Mangus could not fight any more, but he was ashamed to walk away without a good excuse.
"It's too dark to fight any more today," he said gruffly.

Naja's mouth opened a little in the beginnings of a smile. "Good night, then," she said, "and be careful crossing the stream."

Naja was tired too and longed to coil up and go to sleep.
Mangus limped off toward his home in the cane fields.

When Mangus reached the stream, he stopped to drink the cold, sparkling water. He looked at the stones placed in the stream for the cane workers to walk across. They were dangerously far apart.

He leaped to the first stone safely. Then he had to rest before going on. Each stone seemed twice as hard to reach as the last one. It was dark now, and the swift current sounded angry.

Mangus heard a twig snap in the bushes. Frightened, he jumped.

Mangus dug his claws into the slimy moss that grew on the stone. His hind legs and half his body were under water, and the current was pulling him down. He shrieked as the water tore his claws out of the moss and carried him under.

The next thing Mangus knew, he was lying on the bank. He shook his head and tried to breathe. He was surprised to find himself looking into Naja's face. "You were so tired, I thought you might need some help," Naja said.

"Help!" Mangus said bitterly, and shook more water from his nose. "I would have landed on the stone if you hadn't made that noise in the bushes and scared me. Why didn't you let me drown?"

"Who would I fight with? Life would be so dull if I didn't have our battles to look forward to," Naja said.

One sunny day, Mangus came upon Naja lying under the cotton tree.
"At last we meet again," Naja said.
Mangus did not answer. He scratched the ground with his sharp claws and hurled himself at Naja.

They fought and fought and fought—except when Mangus had a cold, or Naja was changing her skin, or when the rainy season came. And during that time they began to become friends. They teased each other and sometimes even laughed at each other.

One morning when Mangus came to Naja's tree, he saw two strangers stuffing a hissing, fighting snake into a basket. It was Naja.

They quickly closed the basket and fastened the catch. Naja had been captured. Mangus silently followed the men through the cane fields to the mansion on the hill.

The men put the basket in the corner of the coach house and slammed the door.

"Well, we've finally done it. We've captured the last snake in Jamaica," one of the strangers said. "She'll make a marvelous exhibit."
Mangus lay down quietly beside the coach house, watching and listening.

When he was sure that everyone had gone away, he climbed through a broken board and came softly to the basket.

"Naja," he called in a whisper.

"Is that you, Mangus?" Naja asked.

"I'll have you out in a minute," Mangus said, as he began to gnaw at the basket.

Quickly, Mangus' sharp teeth bit through the catch. Naja was in such a hurry to get out that she had been pushing her head against the top of the basket and suddenly shot several feet into the air as Mangus released the catch.

Naja crawled swiftly onto the ground and stretched herself to her full length, as if she wanted to make sure that she was all there.

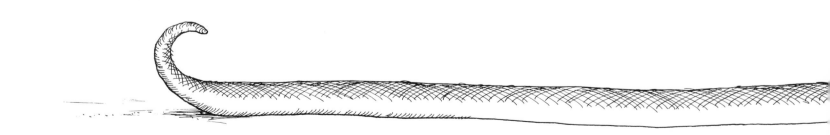

"That was close," she said.
"Let's get away from here as fast as we can," Mangus said.

"We're even with one another now," Mangus said. "You saved my life and I've saved yours. I feel much better. Now I'll be able to fight as if I really mean it."

"Haven't you meant it all along?" Naja asked, smiling.

"Not since you saved my life," Mangus said. "It seemed wrong to kill you when I owed my life to you."

"You might kill yourself trying to kill me," Naja said slyly.

"We'll see," Mangus said. "You'd better stay away from your home under the cotton tree. They'll be looking for you in the morning."

"You're quite right," Naja said. "I'll turn off here and hide in that stand of green cane for a few days. I'll meet you back at the tree when things have quieted down. 'Bye."

The men had given up hope of finding Naja and gone away. Mangus and Naja started fighting all over again. They fought for years and years. They were growing old, and their fights became shorter and less fierce.

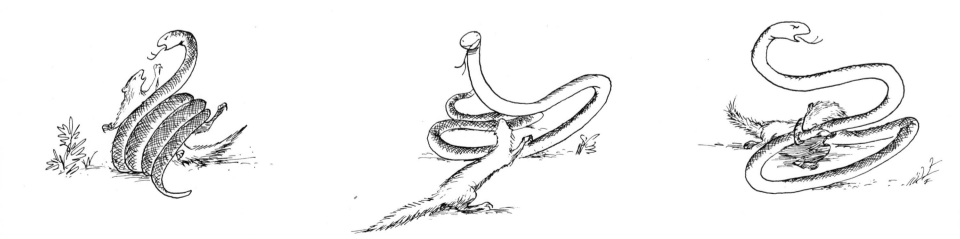

One morning Naja was lying in a shaft of sunlight.
"I'm cold," Mangus said.
"Come and lie beside me, Mangus. We'll keep each other warm," said Naja.
Mangus crawled forward until he was right next to Naja. He trusted her. She had been honorable all through the years of their fighting. And once she had saved his life.

Mangus wriggled and scratched the ground until he was comfortable. Naja lay very still.

"Thank you, Naja," Mangus said, as he leaned himself against Naja's coils. The huge snake unwound her coils and then curled herself again until Mangus was completely surrounded. Then she left her head slide down into the dark where Mangus lay. They both fell asleep at once.

They didn't know that the two men from the zoo were watching them.
Through the years, the men had come back from time to time to look for Naja
but had never been able to find her. Mangus had always heard them long before they came near and warned Naja. His ears had been sharp and keen. But
now, at his age, he was almost completely deaf.

One of the men from the zoo moved toward them on tip toe until he was near enough to throw a strong net over Naja and Mangus. Neither of them stirred.

Gently the men put Naja and Mangus into a basket.

"We'll go back to the zoo at once," one of the men said, "before the snake has a chance to escape again. I never thought I'd see a snake and a mongoose lie down together!"

When the men reached the zoo, they put Mangus and Naja into a large, airy cage. The sunlight kept them toasty warm as they lay beside each other.

All the children came, and their parents too, to look at the marvel of a snake and a mongoose lying beside one another.

Mangus and Naja laughed at their good fortune. Who would have thought they would have such a luxurious old age? They ate and they slept and paid no attention to the people who came to gape at them.

That's how it was with Naja the Snake and Mangus the Mongoose.